TEC

KALEIDOSCOPE

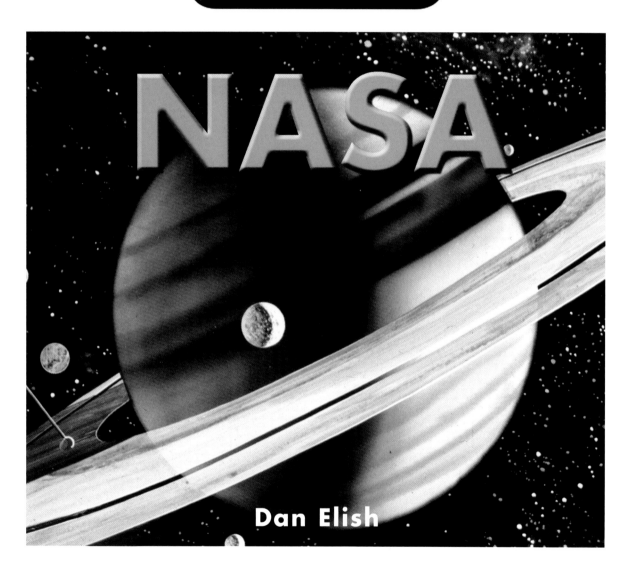

NASA

Dan Elish

 **Marshall Cavendish**
Benchmark
New York

Marshall Cavendish Benchmark
99 White Plains Road
Tarrytown, New York 10591-9001
www.marshallcavendish.us

Library of Congress Cataloging-in-Publication Data
Elish, Dan.
NASA / by Dan Elish.
p. cm. — (Kaleidoscope)
Includes bibliographical references and index.
ISBN-13: 978-0-7614-2046-0 (alk. paper)
ISBN-10: 0-7614-2046-0 (alk. paper)
1. United States. National Aeronautics and Space Administration—Juvenile literature. 2. Outer space—Exploration—United States—Juvenile literature. 3. Astronautics—United States—Juvenile literature. I. Title. II. Series: Kaleidoscope (Tarrytown, N.Y.)
TL521.312.E45 2006   629.4'0973—dc22   2005017279

Editor: Marilyn Mark
Editorial Director: Michelle Bisson
Art Director: Anahid Hamparian
Series Designer: Adam Mietlowski

Photo Research by Anne Burns Images
Cover Photo by NASA

The photographs in this book are used with permission and through the courtesy of: Photri-Microstock: pp. 1, 7, 11, 12, 15, 24, 27, 35 Sovfoto: pp. 4 Tass, 8 JPL / NASA: pp. 16, 19, 20, 36, 39, 40 NASA: pp. 23, 31, 32 JSC Corbis: p. 28, 43 Robert Galbraithe/Reuters

Printed in Malaysia

6 5 4 3 2 1

Contents

Space Race

In the late 1950s the United States and the Soviet Union (now Russia) were the two most powerful nations in the world. Each wanted to be the first country to send a person into space. On October 4, 1957, the Soviets launched *Sputnik*, the world's first *satellite*. A month later, the Soviets launched *Sputnik 2*, which carried the world's first live space traveler—a dog named Laika.

The Soviet Union's success worried many Americans. On July 29, 1958, President Dwight D. Eisenhower signed a bill that set up NASA, the National Aeronautics and Space Administration. NASA's mission was clear: to fly a manned spacecraft out of Earth's *atmosphere* and safely through space.

◄ *The world's first live space traveler, Laika the space dog, sits in the* Sputnik 2 *capsule.*

Project Mercury

To achieve its goal, NASA needed *astronauts*, or people who travel in space. After a search of test pilots from the Army, Air Force, Marine Corps, and Navy, NASA picked seven men: Alan B. Shepard Jr., Virgil I. Grissom, John H. Glenn Jr., M. Scott Carpenter, Walter M. Schirra Jr., L. Gordon Cooper Jr., and Donald K. Slayton. They were chosen to be part of a program called Project Mercury. For the next few years, these men went through flight and survival training. Meanwhile an engineer named Dr. Wernher von Braun developed the *Redstone*, a rocket that would fit under a Mercury capsule and lift the astronauts into space.

The launch of the Mercury-Redstone 2 *capsule, seen here in Cape Canaveral, Florida, was one in a series of flights to prepare American astronauts for manned orbital flights. It carried a chimpanzee named Ham.*

But despite the astronauts' hard work and that of von Braun and his team, NASA couldn't catch up with the Soviets. On April 12, 1961, a *cosmonaut*—the Russian term for "astronaut"—named Major Yuri A. Gagarin made one complete *orbit*, or revolution, around Earth in his ship, *Vostok 1*. Gagarin became an international hero, but NASA wasn't about to give up on Project Mercury.

◀ *Yuri A. Gagarin, cosmonaut for the Soviet Union, is seen here in the* Vostok I *capsule before making his historic orbit around Earth as the first man in space.*

On May 5, 1961, Alan B. Shepard Jr. flew the small spacecraft *Freedom 7* into outer space and landed in the Atlantic Ocean fifteen minutes later. Americans were thrilled. Twenty days later, President John F. Kennedy gave a speech that shocked the world. "I believe," he said, "that this nation should commit itself to achieving the goal, before this decade is out, of landing a man on the Moon and returning him safely to Earth."

President John F. Kennedy shakes the hand of astronaut Alan B. Shepard Jr. ▶
on the White House lawn in a ceremony to honor Shepard's ride in the
Freedom 7 *spacecraft. Shepard was the first American in space.*

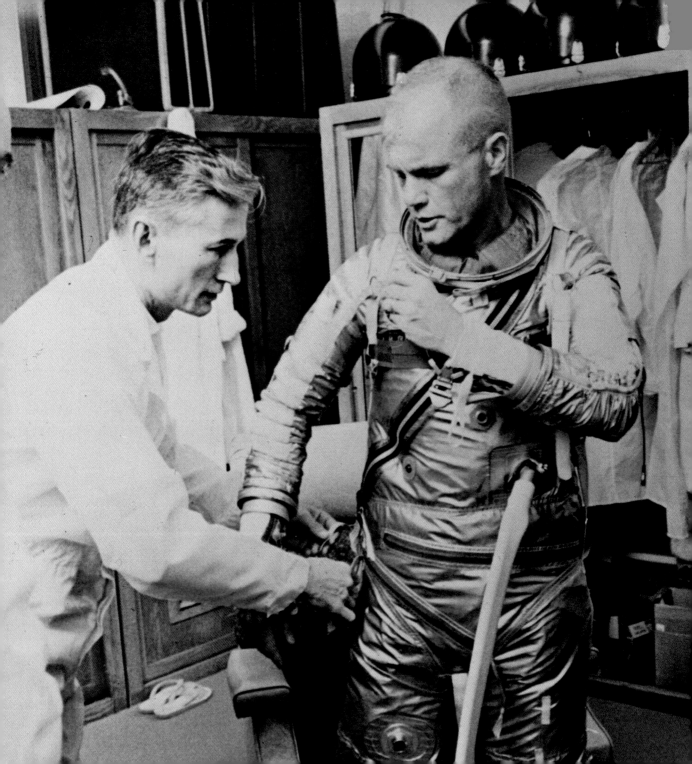

With this goal in mind, work on Project Mercury continued. On February 20, 1962, John H. Glenn Jr. became the first American to orbit Earth. John Glenn's flight—and safe landing in the Atlantic Ocean after near disaster—turned him into a national hero. There were more Mercury launches after that. Each was a success, and America began to pull ahead of the Soviet Union in the space race.

It was time for NASA to focus on President Kennedy's goal: to reach the Moon.

Astronaut John Glenn Jr., the first American to orbit Earth, suits up in preparation for the Mercury *flight. Project Mercury helped the United States catch up to the Soviets in the space race.*

Project Gemini

The successes of the six Mercury flights taught NASA how to launch a spacecraft and control it while in flight. With this knowledge, the NASA team developed a new spacecraft three times the size of the Mercury craft, called Gemini. On March 23, 1965, astronauts Gus Grissom and John W. Young took *Gemini 3* on a test drive. They orbited Earth three times. Unlike the Mercury craft, the Gemini spacecraft had hatches built above the astronauts. These hatches allowed for *EVA* (extra-vehicular activity), through which the astronauts could leave the craft and move around in space. On June 3, 1965, Edward H. White became the first American to go on a *space walk*. By the end of 1966, NASA felt ready to test its new ships.

Edward H. White was the first American to go on a space walk. ▶

Project Apollo

NASA engineers worked hard to find the best way to get to the Moon. They decided to place a small spacecraft called a *lunar module*, or LM, inside a larger rocket, or *command module*. Three astronauts would fly the command module toward the Moon. Once they were safely orbiting it, one astronaut would stay with the command module while the other two would fly the LM down to the *lunar surface*. The plan was called Project Apollo.

◄ *The lunar module of* Apollo 9 *makes its orbit around the Moon.*

Unfortunately, the project's first manned test flight ended in tragedy. A fire in the *capsule* killed all three astronauts. Soon after, tragedy struck the Soviet space program. The cosmonaut Vladimir Komarov died when the ship crash-landed. Neither the United States nor the Soviet Union attempted a manned flight for a year and a half after the accidents. During that time, NASA changed and improved the Apollo command module and began tests on the *Saturn V*, a rocket powerful enough to send Apollo to the Moon.

Finally, NASA was ready to begin manned flights again. In December 1968, *Apollo 8* circled the Moon ten times, then came back to Earth. *Apollo 9* and *Apollo 10* also circled the Moon, and the astronauts test-drove the LM. Then came the most famous Apollo flight of all.

In Apollo 9 *and* Apollo 10, *astronauts test-drove the lunar module (LM) as they orbited the Moon. Shown here is the interior of the LM of* Apollo 9.

On July 16, 1969, Neil Armstong, Buzz Aldrin, and Michael Collins blasted off on *Apollo 11*. Armstrong and Aldrin got into the LM, code-named *Eagle*, on July 20 and headed for the Moon's surface. As Collins kept the command ship, *Columbia*, in orbit, Armstrong and Aldrin flew toward the Sea of Tranquility, a lunar plain. Armstrong steered the LM away from a giant crater and safely landed. He made history as the first man to set foot on the Moon, saying the famous words, "That's one small step for man, one giant leap for mankind." America had answered President Kennedy's challenge.

Other Apollo missions followed. American astronauts collected moon rocks and studied the lunar surface. In total, six NASA spacecraft reached the Moon's surface. Twelve astronauts walked on the Moon.

◀ *Astronaut Buzz Aldrin stands in front of the American flag after the successful* Apollo 11 *flight into space.*

Skylab

NASA now turned its attention to setting up a permanent station in space. In 1973 NASA used its powerful Saturn rockets to launch *Skylab*, a space station designed to orbit Earth for eight to ten years. In its first year in orbit, three separate crews lived in *Skylab*. The first crew spent twenty-eight days in space; the second spent fifty-nine days; and the third spent eighty-four days. In total, the *Skylab* astronauts stayed in space longer than the astronauts of all Soviet and American space flights up to that time combined. *Skylab* proved that longer manned missions were possible, and the astronauts' experience taught NASA scientists a great deal about the effects of space travel on human health.

In this artist's rendering, we see the Skylab *space station as it circles Earth,* ▶
with its twin pole thermal shield deployed to shade it from the Sun.

The Apollo-Soyuz Test Project

The Apollo-Soyuz Test Project marked the first time that the American and Soviet space programs worked together. The project was designed to test how well American and Soviet spacecraft could join together, or dock, in space.

On July 17, 1975, a Soviet Soyuz craft and an American Apollo craft went into orbit around Earth and docked successfully. Soviet and American astronauts were able to pass back and forth between the two craft through a special module built by NASA engineers. The crews performed a variety of experiments, and after two days the Soyuz craft and the Apollo craft separated successfully. Apollo-Soyuz showed that international space rescue was possible.

◀ *Today, many countries are working together in space. Shown here is the International Space Station (ISS) after assembly was completed in 2003. The ISS is a collaboration of sixteen countries that shows what can be achieved when countries work together rather than compete.*

Space Shuttle

In 1981 NASA introduced *Columbia*, a *space shuttle*, to the world. It was the first craft designed to take off like a rocket and land on a runway like an airplane. On April 12, 1981, *Columbia* began its first successful flight. It orbited Earth thirty-six times, and afterward its crew landed the shuttle safely at Edwards Air Force Base near Lancaster, California.

Columbia's success was a major step forward for NASA. Although the Apollo rockets had performed well, they could only be used once. Now NASA had a spacecraft that could be used again and again.

The Columbia *space shuttle at liftoff.* Columbia *could take off like a rocket and land like an airplane, making it the first-ever reusable spacecraft.* ▶

Over the next five years, three other shuttles, *Challenger, Discovery,* and *Atlantis,* also made successful flights. But on January 28, 1986, *Challenger* met with disaster. The craft burst into flames one minute after takeoff, killing all seven crew members.

NASA stopped all shuttle flights while engineers investigated the cause of the disaster. Once the problem was identified and fixed in the other shuttles, a new shuttle, *Endeavor,* was built to replace *Challenger* in the shuttle fleet.

◀ *Four crew members of the space shuttle* Challenger *sit in the shuttle mission simulator. From left: Michael J. Smith, Ellison S. Onizuka, Judith A. Resnik, and Francis R. (Dick) Scobee. All seven crew members, including Ronald E. McNair, Gregory B. Jarvis, and Christa McAuliffe (not shown here), were killed when the craft burst into flames shortly after takeoff.*

In the 1990s astronauts in the shuttles flew many successful missions. Missions included satellite launches and the repair of satellites already in orbit. Shuttle crews also performed a variety of scientific tests and studies, including studies of the effect of space on the Sun's rays, plant growth, and aging, and studies of new materials for use in electronic devices. On February 1, 2003, disaster struck again. Streaking through the atmosphere on its way back to Earth, the shuttle *Columbia* broke apart. All seven astronauts were lost. NASA later discovered that the disaster had been caused by a damaged wing. NASA engineers made improvements meant to prevent future shuttle disasters.

Astronauts often have to make repairs to space shuttles and other equipment. Here, astronaut Michael J. Massimino works on the Hubble Telescope's port side solar array.

▶

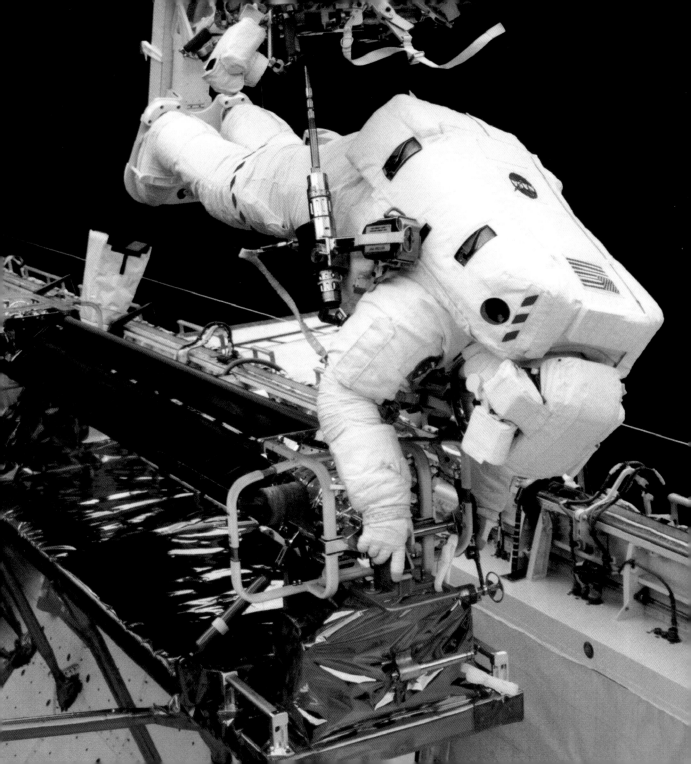

Exploring the Galaxy

Some of NASA's greatest achievements have come through the use of unmanned spacecraft. In the 1970s NASA began building a giant telescope that could orbit Earth. Working with European astronomers, NASA built the *Hubble Space Telescope*, named after astronomer Edwin Powell Hubble. In 1990 the Hubble Space Telescope was launched into orbit with high hopes. But within a few months, scientists learned that the telescope wasn't focused properly. In December 1993 astronauts aboard *Endeavor* made a series of daring space walks and fixed Hubble's lens. Almost immediately the telescope began to show astronomers beautiful pictures of the galaxy!

◀ *The Hubble Space Telescope, launched in 1990, was not focused properly. In 1993 astronauts fixed its lens.*

NASA has also launched unmanned spacecraft that have traveled to the Moon, Mars, and other parts of the Solar System. Launched in the early 1970s, *Pioneer 10* and *Pioneer 11* flew past Jupiter and Saturn. With scientific tools and cameras, the probes gathered important information about these planets.

This artwork shows the Pioneer 11 *spacecraft flying past Saturn. The spacecraft was the second to investigate Jupiter and the outer Solar System and the first to explore Saturn and its main rings. On September 1, 1979, the craft passed by Saturn at a distance of 13,049 miles (21,000 km) from Saturn's cloud tops.*

On November 7, 1996, NASA launched the *Mars Global Surveyor*. It has been in orbit around Mars since 1997. On July 4, 1997, a small craft called the *Mars Pathfinder* actually landed on the Red Planet. It explored the surface with a miniature vehicle, or rover, called *Sojourner*, and gave NASA scientists and the world amazing pictures of the Martian landscape.

In the summer of 2003, NASA launched *Spirit* and *Opportunity*, two new Mars rovers. On January 3, 2004, *Spirit* touched down on the surface of Mars. *Opportunity* landed on January 24 on a different part of the planet. Each probe traveled about 44 yards (40 meters) a day, which is more than the *Sojourner* traveled in its entire mission.

◄ *The* Mars Pathfinder *spacecraft entered the Martian atmosphere without going into orbit around the Red Planet, and landed with the aid of parachutes, rockets, and airbags, as shown in this artist's rendering. The* Pathfinder *took atmospheric measurements before touching down on the surface.*

The rovers took pictures of the Martian surface and ran tests on rocks and soil. In early March 2004, NASA scientists concluded from the rovers' data that part of Mars was once covered with water—and so could once have been home to a variety of life forms.

On October 15, 1997, a spacecraft called *Cassini-Huygens* was launched toward Saturn. After traveling 2.2 billion miles (3.5 billion km), the spacecraft entered Saturn's orbit on June 30, 2004. For the first time in history, scientists saw images of the ringed planet and its thirty-one moons close up. *Cassini-Huygens* continues to give scientists more information about the planets in our Solar System.

Shown here is a model of the Sojourner *rover, the vehicle that traveled the Martian landscape, taking pictures and conducting experiments on Martian rocks and soil.*

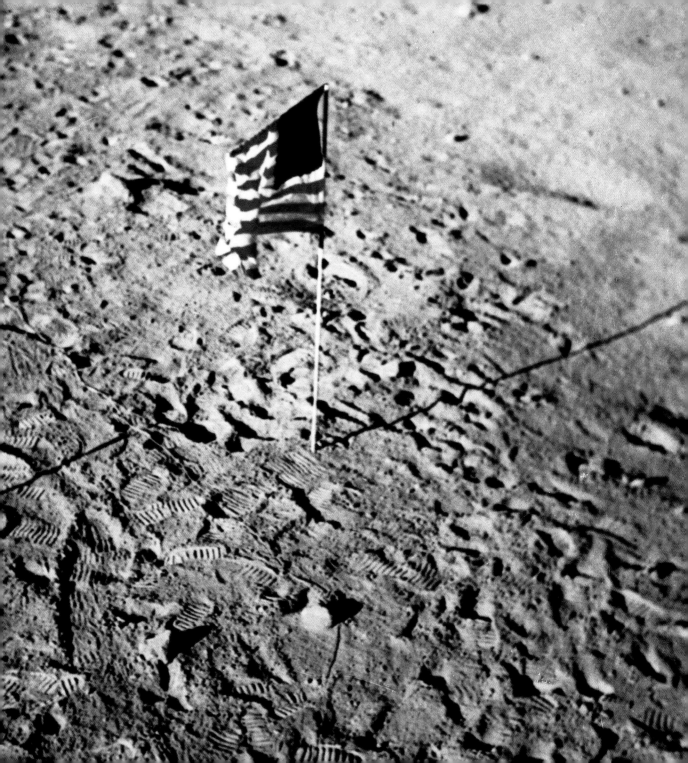

NASA in the Future

On January 14, 2004, President George W. Bush delivered a speech about NASA, calling for more manned missions to explore space. He urged NASA to return astronauts to the Moon on long-term missions by the year 2020. He suggested that a lasting presence on the Moon could pave the way for manned missions to Mars and beyond. At the end of his speech, the president explained why space travel is important:

Mankind is drawn to the heavens for the same reason we were once drawn into unknown lands and across the open sea. We choose to explore space because doing so improves our lives and lifts our national spirit.

President George W. Bush urged NASA to return astronauts to the Moon on long-term missions by the year 2020. Exploring space has been a national goal since the 1950s.

NASA's focus on sending men and women to the Moon is similar to the aim set by President Kennedy in 1961, though NASA is no longer involved in a space race. NASA does have a new competitor—private industry. On October 4, 2004, *SpaceShipOne*, a rocket ship made by the company Scaled Composites won the $10 million Ansari X Prize. The prize was offered to any privately funded spaceship that could carry a pilot and the weight of two passengers to an altitude of nearly 70 miles (113 km), NASA's designated "boundary of space" within two weeks. But a day after *SpaceShipOne*'s victory, NASA raised the official boundary of space to 150 miles (241 km) above the Earth's surface.

SpaceShipOne, *shown here with Pilot Brian Binnie atop, became the first privately funded manned spaceship to reach the edge of suborbital space—and claim the $10 million Ansari X Prize.*

Glossary

astronaut—A person who travels in space.

astronomer—Someone who studies the planets, stars, and other objects in space.

atmosphere—The air around a planet or moon.

capsule—A small, pressurized compartment in a rocket.

cosmonaut—The Russian term for "astronaut."

extra-vehicular activity (EVA)—When an astronaut exits a spacecraft to go on a space walk or to perform some other activity.

Hubble Space Telescope—A powerful device that is in orbit around Earth. It is used to record images of distant galaxies.

lunar module (LM)—The small ship used by Apollo astronauts to fly between their spacecraft and the Moon.

lunar surface—The surface of the Moon.

orbit—The path a planet follows as it circles its local star, or that a moon or spacecraft follows around a planet.

satellite—Either a humanmade object such as a spacecraft, or a natural space object such as a moon, that orbits a larger body.

space shuttle—The first reusable spacecraft. It is able to take off like a rocket and land like an airplane.

space walk—When an astronaut exits a spacecraft either to make a repair or to explore.

Find Out More

Books

Baird, Anne. *The U.S. Space Camp Book of Astronauts*. New York: Morrow Junior Books, 1996.

Bean, Alan. *Apollo*. Shelton, CT: Greenwich Workshop Press, 1998.

Bergreen, Laurence. *Voyage to Mars: NASA's Search For Life Beyond Earth*. New York: Riverhead Books, 2000.

Hehner, Barbara. *First on the Moon*. New York: Hyperion Books for Children, 1999.

Johnstone, Michael. *In Space*. Cambridge, MA: Candlewick Press, 1999.

Kerrod, Robin. *The Illustrated History of NASA*. New York: Gallery Books, 1986.

Sipiera, Diane M., and Paul P. Sipiera. *Project Mercury*. New York: Children's Press, 1997.

Vogt, Gregory. *A Twenty-fifth Anniversary Album of NASA*. New York: Franklin Watts, 1983.

Web Sites

The Apollo Missions
http://www.lpi.usra.edu/expmoon/apollo_landings.html
http://www.nasm.edu/apollo/apollo.htm

Hubble Space Telescope
http://hubblesite.org/gallery
http://oposite.stsci.edu/

Information from the Kennedy Space Center
http://www.ksc.nasa.gov/

NASA homepage
http://www.nasa.gov/

NASA for kids
http://kids.msfc.nasa.gov/

Project Mercury
http://www-pao.ksc.nasa.gov/kscpao/history/mercury/mercury.htm

SpaceShipOne
http://www.scaled.com/projects/tierone/
http://watleyreview.com/2004/100504-3.html

About the Author

Dan Elish has written a variety of fiction and nonfiction books for children, including *The Trail of Tears: The Story of the Cherokee Removal*, hailed as an "excellent resource" by *School Library Journal*. He also wrote *Born Too Short, The Confessions of an 8th Grade Basket Case*, which was picked as a Book for the Teen Age in 2003 by the New York Public Library, and also won a 2004 International Reading Association Students' Choice Award. Dan is also an accomplished television script writer. He lives in New York City with his wife and daughter.

Index